Definitely it was the eyes:

Faded blue, they were, with a hint of things no man and surely no woman was meant to see.

"Your husband around?" the rider asked when his eyes had rejoined mine.

"Inside," I answered.

He weighed that. Twin Peacemakers in an oiled double holster, the butter-colored handle of something smaller protruding from his belt. Shearling coat with the collar up, gray wool trousers over the dusted boots and unroweled spurs. Tooled saddlebags, brass on the buttplate of his rifle. No farmer, yet something about him that kept my fear at bay.

Barely…

Wind on the River

"The sheer beauty and strength of Barre's writing gives a glow of redemption that is extremely rare in any kind of fiction."

–DICK ADLER
Chicago Tribune

"There is a spooky polish rubbed over all of this, onto every surface until it shines. Barre knows what he is doing and this story shows it. Edgar [Allen Poe] would be proud because it ripples with the muscle of less being more."

–MICHAEL CONNELLY
best-selling author of *The Narrows* and *Lost Light,*
from his Foreword to *The Star*

"Although known as a writer of outstanding detective novels, Richard Barre has written a suspense story of extraordinary poignancy that will keep readers at the edge of their seats as they dry their eyes."

–OTTO PENZLER
The Mysterious Bookshop, New York

"No one has done [a final chance at redemption] better – in any form – than Rod Serling. Richard Barre shows the same depth and humanity that illuminated Serling's work by reminding us – as we question ourselves in bleak moments – of the questions we often forget to ask: Are the switches flipped by chance or design? Are we being given a curse or a gift?"

–ROBERT CRAIS

best-selling author of *The Last Detective* and *L.A. Requiem,* from his foreword to *Bethany*

Other Books by Richard Barre

The Innocents
Bearing Secrets
The Ghosts of Morning
Blackheart Highway
The Star
Burning Moon
Bethany
Echo Bay

Wind on the River

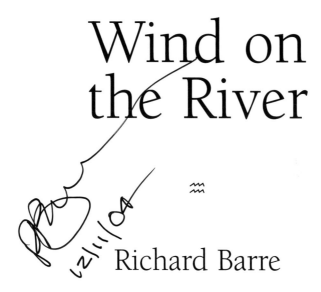

Richard Barre

Foreword by Harlan Coben

CAPRA PRESS
MEMORABLE BOOKS SINCE 1969
SANTA BARBARA

A Robert Bason Book
Published by Capra Press
815 De La Vina Street
Santa Barbara, CA 93101
www.caprapress.com

Cover and book design by Frank Goad
Cover photograph by Frank Goad

Library of Congress Cataloging-in-Publication Data

Barre, Richard.
Wind on the river / Richard Barre ; foreword by Harlan Coben.— 1st ed.
p. cm.
"A Robert Bason book"—T.p. verso.
ISBN 1-59266-045-2 — ISBN 1-59266-046-0 (numbered ed.)
ISBN 1-59266-047-9 (lettered ed.)
1. Outlaws—Fiction. 2. Fugitives from justice—Fiction.
3. Coma—Patients—Fiction. 4. Married women—Fiction.
5. Women farmers—Fiction. 6. South Dakota—Fiction. I. Title.

PS3552.A73253W56 2004
813'.54—dc22
2004005654

Edition: 10 9 8 7 6 5 4 3 2 1

First Edition

Third in the Series

FOREWORD

Harlan Coben

Wow.

I've been trying to come up with a unique way to say this, to express my admiration for this rich tale, to explain the wonderful hair-on-the-arms rising effect certain stories have on the reader, the ones that let you know that what you are experiencing is special, that the words will linger and stay with you and never fully leave you, that the story will rattle inside your chest and that you will be enormously grateful for that feeling.

But the best I can come up with, using the vast reservoir that is my personal vocabulary (and, alas, the computer's thesaurus) is:

Wow.

Wind on the River is billed as a Christmas story. I guess that is so. But with all due respect to Richard Barre, the description is far from full. This is a love story. It is a Western. It is a tale of loyalty, of devotion, of loss and lust, of family, of quiet heroism, of redemption, of want, of healing. But I guess that would be too much to put on the cover.

Richard Barre has long been one of my favorite private-eye writers, but *Wind on the River* demonstrates what an incredible talent he is. Does it show his diversity? Yes, of course. His gift for language and storytelling? Sure. But more than that, Richard Barre's ability to move us in ways both subtle and powerful – that's what raises this story into the realm of greatness.

Greatness. I don't use that word often. But as with "Wow," it works here.

The holidays are, of course, all about tradition. Richard Barre's Christmas stories are fast becoming like well-decorated trees, stockings hung on fireplaces, candles on menorahs, exchanged presents. He has given us all a great gift with *Wind on the River*.

Cherish it.

HARLAN COBEN

March 2004

Wind on the River

Nevada City, California
November 26, 1913

For all I knew, he came with the wind. And as I
take pen to note what happened those many years ago,
I close my eyes and see him still. Across time, the river
mist rising to the trees, the sun I had to raise my hand
against that day. As if my mind had been the very cam-
era that took our wedding picture, Aaron's and mine,
that June day at Fort Sully.

Eight years before *he* appeared…

~~~

Cheyenne River Country
Dakota Territory
December 19, 1879

As I said, there he was. Nothing but riverbend one minute, then him on that dark-maned sorrel roan of his. Like something carved and set down into my field of vision instead of the last of the potatoes I was rooting up, the occasional glance around for Mary Elizabeth clearing Jonathan's grave. Winter late in locking us in its frigid embrace, ice not yet thick enough to walk on in the Cheyenne's shallows, gravel bars poking up like the backs of sturgeon frozen where they'd breached. Bluff country this was, broken chalk tableland, the rivercut acting like a funnel for the wind. The one thing Aaron hadn't taken into account when he'd set our house down where it was. Aaron, ever the dreamer.

But I stray.

"Thought for a minute you was cavalry," the rider said as I aimed a squint up at him. No time to be alarmed, though Lord knows there was cause. Us near thirty miles from Spurlock, another hundred-plus from Fort Sully. Hawks and sky and river and rolling prairie grass bent to the wind. Aaron's idea to live out here, a concession to me, though he never said it outright.

"A cavalry soldier rooting out potatoes," I came back. "There would be a sight."

"Must have been the trousers," he said. No expression and not much more in the way of movement. Weathered tan, hat and boots showing a layer of fine white dust. "Not every day I encounter a woman in stripers."

"They'd be my husband's," I told him, hoping it might transfer some of the unease I was starting to feel now. For despite the banter, he was like none I'd seen among the farmers and merchants of Spurlock, who still expected the railroad to divert their way and make them rich. No, the closest might have been the Army scouts I'd known, hawk-eyed veterans of a thousand frontier skirmishes.

Definitely it was the eyes: Faded blue, they were, with a hint of things no man and surely no woman was meant to see. Eyes that took in the barn and house soon as I mentioned Aaron, the old dugout we'd first built from sod and now used as a root cellar, the corral where a few of our mares nickered at the roan. The knoll where Mary Elizabeth had ceased her weeding and stood watching, not sure what to do, but awaiting my signal.

And what was I up to during all this looking around? Wishing I were nearer Aaron's Winchester or his New Model Army .44, both of which I took pride in knowing how to shoot. Two wolf-pelt throws and Aaron's buffalo robe testament to that.

"Your husband around?" the rider asked when his eyes had rejoined mine.

"Inside," I answered.

He weighed that. Twin Peacemakers in an oiled double holster, the butter-colored handle of something smaller protruding from his belt. Shearling coat with the collar up, gray wool trousers over the dusted boots and unroweled spurs. Tooled saddlebags, brass on the buttplate of his rifle. No farmer, yet something about him that kept my fear at bay.

Barely.

"Who's up the knoll there?" he said at length.

"My daughter."

"I meant the grave."

"My son," I told him, feeling the earth in my hands again. Hearing it hit the homemade coffin as Aaron shoveled as gently as he could to spare me, though nothing ever would. "Croup took him last winter."

"I'm sorry," he said, seeming to mean it. "How old?"

"Jonathan was seven."

The eyes left me, came back. "And your daughter?"

"Mary Elizabeth's five, thank you."

We stood there until I felt Mary Elizabeth tug at my horse-blanket coat and looked down to see her sizing up the stranger.

"Hello, Mary Elizabeth," he said down to her.

"Hello." Right back, a bit like me in her directness. Something less than a virtue, often enough.

"Take the potatoes and go inside, Mary Elizabeth. Tell your father we have company."

She looked at me strangely. "But mama. Papa is—"

"*Now, Mary Elizabeth,*" I said a bit too sharply, and when she'd taken off for the house regretted.

"Papa is what?" the stranger inquired. "Besides once being a Union cavalryman and lending you his trousers."

"You are bold, aren't you?"

A gust took his reply. Something to do with time.

"My husband is in the house," I said, not altogether convincingly because of the way he regarded me. "Convalescing," I added, hoping that would stick.

The flicker in his expression passed, leaving more fatigue than curiosity. "I saw your horses," he said.

"Mine's rode out. Mind if I water and feed him?"

"I suppose not."

"It wasn't meant to take advantage. I can pay."

"That won't be necessary. But we are not a rest stop. My husband and I raise horses for the fort." And whoever else will pay us for them, I thought but didn't say.

"Ma'am, we pause only of necessity," he said, dismounting gingerly. "My name is John Smith. This here's Bob Lee."

"Laney...Van Rensslaer," I said. "My husband is Aaron of the Missouri Van Rensslaers whose regiment acquitted themselves with Chamberlain and against Bloody Bill Anderson in the later stages before coming west to forts Laramie and Sully." Too proudly, I knew, but wanting him to know who he was dealing with. You see I was anything but sure about him. Just showing up like that, miles from Spurlock and anywhere else for that matter. Wind popping like the keelboat's mainsail when it put in a week ago on its monthly stop.

"The war...yes, ma'am," he said. Letting Bob Lee make for the trough, he fumbled in a pocket, came out with a double-eagle he held out to me. "For the use of your barn. Two souls."

I hesitated. Twenty dollars.

And yet, under the circumstances...

"For Bob Lee, if not myself."

Bob Lee did look exhausted, though no more so than his rider.

"Two souls," I agreed, palming the gold piece after an appropriate pause.

We saw no more of either of them that day.

〜〜〜

December 20, 1879

As it was Sunday, we spent the morning reading the Bible around Aaron's bed after I'd fed and bathed him. In the spirit, I'd had Mary Elizabeth put a portion of our breakfast inside the barn door. Nothing fancy, biscuits and gravy, a few pennies measured against the double eagle. I was reading Luke 15:11-32, the Prodigal, when I heard the floorboards creak, and there stood John Smith, my empty plate in his hand. Too amazed to address this presumption, I merely sat as his eyes took in Aaron, Mary Elizabeth in her Sunday dress, me in mine.

Then the doorway was empty.

When we'd regained ourselves and changed clothes, we heard an axe. I bade Mary Elizabeth continue her Bible reading, such as she'd been able to master, which was quite accomplished for age five, if I say so myself, then went outside to find him by the shed. Shirt off, a strong sun for little more than freezing beating down on his back. Already he'd blocked out about a quarter of a cord. Sweat ran from his hair and glistened on his skin. Propped against the side of the barn was his rifle and, over a post, his double holster.

For a moment I watched, then I said, "At this house, we observe the Lord's day, Mr. Smith."

He spoke as if knowing I'd been there all the time, though I was quiet in my approach. "And his son wasn't born in the Dakotas, Mrs. Van Rensslaer. I doubt he expects the same adherence this time of year."

I felt a flush rise. "You're very–"

"Bold. I know." *Chop.*

"Mary Elizabeth and I can stack that tomorrow."

"Thank you for the breakfast," he said, splitting another log.

"The least I could do for what it bought."

Not knowing whether to get back to Mary Elizabeth or attempt further intercession on behalf of the Lord, I compromised. "Bob Lee need salt lick or liniment?"

Chop. "Other than a romp with those mares of yours, Bob Lee's about as happy as he's been for a while."

"Then I expect you'll be moving on."

"I will at that, Mrs. Van Rensslaer."

"And may I ask where you're headed?"

"You may." *Chop.*

I waited, as he picked up another log and positioned it, but no destination was offered. Finally he said, "Why's your husband like that?"

"As I mentioned, my husband is convalescing," I answered coolly. "Mornings he spends in bed."

Chop.

"You folks know what you're doing out here?"

"I'm sure I don't know what you mean, Mr. Smith. And I'll have your respect when you address me."

"Believe me, it's yours, ma'am. How long has he been like that?"

"My affair, if it's all the same to you."

I'd turned and was making for the house when he said, "A girl of five and a husband who stares at the ceiling?"

"Mary Elizabeth is almost six and of great help. And now we'll thank you to be on your way."

He brought the axe down, left the blade angled in the block. He'd picked up his shirt and guns and was making for the barn when I felt Mary Elizabeth's scream like an arrow.

~~~

The knife Mary Elizabeth had been using to etch holly and letters into a split and flattened lard can was an apple corer I hadn't seen in years. Somehow she'd dug it up and nearly severed three of her fingers with it. The blood had to be as terrifying as the pain because there she was when I threw back the door, bouncing around the kitchen, smearing everything she touched.

"It was for you," she kept wailing. *"For Christmas. Ow, ow, ow, ow, ow."*

"Mary Elizabeth, look at me, you're all right," I tried to distract her. But she was impossible to hold and less so to convince, wild and slippery. That is until John Smith caught and held her to him.

"You need to stop the bleeding," he said, gripping her wrist as blood poured off the hand. Wrapping it in his shirt while she moaned, her eyes wide with fear.

With the pressure John Smith applied, the bleeding

slowed, and I got after needle and thread. Finally I made the eye and went to work, my child screaming with each new jab. I was making a mess of it, losing my grip and feeling each inept stitch myself, cursing her struggles, when in a steady voice he bade us switch. I protested, I'm sure I did. But her hysteria settled it and I relinquished the needle and set about calming her.

To my amazement the stitching was done then and he directed me to wrap it, which I did, though blood persisted in places. For a while we just sat, Mary Elizabeth keening and John Smith telling her how brave she'd been and how he'd seen grown men cry out far worse for their mamas. Finally the whiskey and milk and honey took hold and she nodded off.

As he laid her in bed, I elevated her bandaged hand on pillows. "Thank you," I told him.

"I'd clean it every day, not to tell you your business."

"May I ask where you acquired such a skill?"

"Man picks up what he picks up," was all he answered. Which was fine by me, nothing wrong with not filling the air with words. Women did enough of that, heaven knew, especially town women. But after I'd set to in the kitchen with towels and water, John Smith nodded at our bedroom, Aaron's and mine, and said,

"He doesn't hear, either?"

"Not in the usual sense."

"What did it?"

Not quite sure why, I told him. How Aaron, while in town on one of his infrequent trips, had been goaded into a fight. How one of the men who beat him finished it with a pick handle. How Aaron had made no sound since, Doc Stroebel, when he brought Aaron back, merely shaking his head and telling me to keep him comfortable. That he could slip away or come out of it, there was no way of telling. About the guilt I felt when it got to be too much and I'd have to go down to the river and scream, the wind taking it like the wolf calls we heard on moonlit nights.

All of it pouring out like the Cheyenne in flood.

"How is it he sustains life?" John Smith asked.

"He'll swallow what I put up to him. That reflex still works." As does what comes with it, I thought but didn't add.

"And you've managed out here?"

"The horses even out. Aaron's pension helps."

"Ever think of moving to town?"

"We quite like it here, thank you," I said, too rapidly. For a while John Smith said nothing. Then, "What

Richard Barre

are you, Mrs. Van Rensslaer, twenty-four?"

"Twenty-six. What difference does that make?"

"Hard not to notice how much closer you are to my age than his."

Anger flared in me. "I will tolerate no such talk of my husband. Aaron saved me from something far worse than death, if you know anything of loneliness and melancholy. He is the kindest man I ever knew."

He finished his coffee and, almost as an afterthought, said, "The fight was over you, wasn't it?"

I nearly dropped my cup.

"No joy being an outcast among your own people, is it?"

He stood, Mary Elizabeth's blood close to set on his shirt. "The tattoo on your neck," he added. "Sioux or Northern Cheyenne, if I had to guess." Then, glancing out at the river, "Bob Lee and I are much obliged for the hospitality. We can still make time."

He was almost to the door when I blurted, "Mr. Smith, wait. At least let me soak out your shirt." Despite my flare-up and subsequent astonishment, feeling more than beholden for his assistance. "Aaron has one you can put on while it dries. Meantime, I'll start supper. That way you can start fresh at daylight."

From the way he stiffened I thought my words had fallen on deaf ears. Until I realized that something out the window had brought him up short. Without turning from it he said, "You really want to help, go to the barn and unsaddle Bob Lee. Pile hay over the saddle and turn him out among your mares. You can tell them you traded one of yours for him. That I lit out west."

"Why would I do that? Tell who?"

"Them," he said, pointing to the column of dust.

∿

Barely had I finished when their horses topped the rise and plunged into the river, arriving in my yard still dripping. Twenty-five or -six of them, fanning out around the leader. Some were in dusters as he was, others in wool or leather coats, all with pistols on their hips. The leader, who was wearing close-fitting black gloves, was a florid-faced man of perhaps forty. Finished with his initial visual survey, he tipped his hat to me and said, "Mrs. Van Rensslaer?"

"And you would be?" I answered, trying to stay calm.

"Captain William Longstreet. You might have heard

of our agency. The Pinkerton?"

"I have indeed," I responded with more confidence than I felt.

"We're gratified to hear it."

The warmth had fled from the day, leaving the sky tasseled with high white streaks. Standing in the thin light, wishing for my horse blanket, I said, "You'd be the bunch still after the James gang. Lest you caught up the last couple of weeks and the news is late arriving."

They exchanged looks, and I wondered if I hadn't picked too hard at a scab. Eight years and neither Frank nor Jesse in jail, a fact I knew from the keelboat people.

"A matter of time, ma'am," Longstreet assured me. "The Younger contingent is another story. After the failed raid at Northfield, Minnesota, Cole, Bob, and Jim now get their mail in Stillwater pen." He paused to eye the barn again. "But the Youngers are not the reason for this call. Their cousin would be, a murderous killer as ever drew breath. One Jubal Pyne." He spat in the dust. "Not only was he with them at Northfield, three weeks ago he accounted for two of the finest lawmen to wear the badge. Agents Vogel and Pennington, gunned down outside Independence."

"Independence being Missouri."

"Yes, ma'am, and only adding to his total. Recently he was spotted at Fort Pierre. Which would follow because he uses rivers to cover his tracks. We believe that to include the Missouri and now the Cheyenne."

I'd become conscious of one of his lieutenants taking my measure unashamedly. Before I knew it, I'd put a hand to my throat and as quickly removed it.

"And you believe him here?"

"People in Spurlock said you lived along the river. We were hoping you might have seen him." He handed me an illustrated wanted poster and I tried not to gasp. Because there he was, the man in my house, the man I knew as John Smith.

Jubal Pyne.

It even described Bob Lee.

An agent who'd been eyeing the corral eased his horse over, whispered something to Longstreet, and I knew from his look that what I said next was crucial.

"Big as life," I told him, handing it back. "Sold him a mare – forty dollars plus the one he was riding. The roan over there, dark mane? That would be his."

There was a stir among the mounted agents, several edging closer to the barn. Longstreet raised his hand for quiet and, failing to mask the gleam in his eye, asked me when Jubal Pyne had shown himself.

I hesitated, as if in thought, which was every bit the truth.

"Week or more ago," I answered then. "Just came, did his business and left."

"You get a gander at which way?"

"Let me think. West, I believe. Along the river."

"Then you don't mind if we search the barn and the house?"

Though it sent a chill through me, I'd anticipated it and answered, "I'll take you inside. My daughter badly cut herself this afternoon and my husband is also resting."

"Thank you, but we'll handle it. Man like that, you can't be too careful."

They were going to regardless, I knew, so I allowed it, all the while asking myself what in hell I was doing. The risk if it turned bad. But scrutinizing Longstreet and his agents gave me no assurance that Jubal Pyne would return alive in their care, and no matter what he'd done, every man deserved a chance. Then there was Mary Elizabeth. No cold-blooded killer would have held her that way, reassuring when under the circumstances he could have taken what he fancied and left us imperiled.

The man beside Longstreet motioned and two groups peeled off, one toward the house, the other toward the barn and dugout, Longstreet saying, "Our sympathies regarding your husband, ma'am. We learned of his misfortune."

But I was not so easily distracted. "Please tell your men that everything gets left as it is," I replied. "Water and hay, all you want, but three mouths live here."

"You heard the lady," Longstreet called out. "As is."

For the first time, the man beside him spoke, the one who had been appraising me. "That why you live so far out, ma'am? Spurlock not what you'd call partial to white squaws?"

"Who is this man," I demanded of Longstreet.

"Agent Zel Clausen, late of Clay County, Missouri," he said with a glance that might or might not have been judgmental. "Knows Jesse and Frank by sight, he does. Jubal Pyne, as well."

Clausen tipped his hat. "That I do. *Ma'am.*"

"Well, agent Clausen will keep a civil tongue in his head or he will leave this property," I said, my flush no act. "A person's preference for domicile is no concern of his."

Clausen added a smile to his list of sins. "Fact is, I've heard them bucks can smell a white woman ten miles off. You find that true in your experience?"

A snicker went up from the remaining posse. Over the rushing in my ears, I could hear the wind rattling my corn, the fan blades turning above the trough. Finally I bit down and said something like, "Climb down off that horse, Agent Clausen, and see how much you have left to imagine with when I'm done with you."

The smile became an evil grin. "Might just take you up on that – *ma'am*." Looking around for support among his cohorts and, sad to say, finding some.

"That will be enough," Longstreet said, halting the murmur. And to me, "Manners tend not to accompany long rides. They mean no harm."

By now the other agents were back and mounting up, shaking their heads at Longstreet. One came licking sweet potato pie off his fingers. Which ordinarily would have set me off, but in light of Clausen's remark I was able to put in perspective. It also gave me a chance to simmer down and remember what was at stake.

"That said, my offer for hay and water still stands," I told him.

"Much obliged, but I doubt our quarry will be feeding and watering with daylight left." He reined his horse, clucked to it. "Good luck to you this winter, ma'am. And don't worry about the Jubal Pyne's of this world, they're finished. They just don't know it yet."

With a final leer from Clausen, Longstreet led them out of the yard and across the river.

I remember watching their dust plume over the willows.

〜〜〜

The Pinkertons had given Aaron the berth they might a crazed person. Which made Jubal Pyne's decision to take refuge under Aaron's bed a clever one. Yet it troubled me that he'd put Aaron in harm's way, and I told him so in no uncertain terms.

I could see him struggle with the challenge. Finally he said, "I figured the chance of any shooting was lessened by it, ma'am. If I chose wrong, I own up to it."

"Wrong would appear to be your side in more than this instance."

We were at the kitchen table, darkness close about the log house. Mary Elizabeth still sleeping after her ordeal and Jubal Pyne taking frequent peeks at the moonlit river, thinking the Pinkertons could have double-backed a watch, despite my having seen nothing to suggest it.

"Peaceful out here," he said after one such lookout.

"Used to be," I answered.

He broke off a piece of bread and chewed it. "You don't know them, what they're capable of."

"And what are you capable of, *Jubal Pyne*?"

He swallowed. "Like anyone, I suppose I'm finding out."

"Anyone didn't kill Longstreet's agents."

In the silence I could hear the wicks burning in the kerosene lamps, the wind tapping my leafless bushes against the glass.

"Did you?" I asked him directly. "Kill those men?"

"I did, ma'am."

"And you saw fit to bring that into my house."

A weariness seemed to take him. He regarded hands one might assume belonged to a pianist or doctor, not a gunfighter. "I had no idea they were as near or I'd have ridden on. Bob Lee and I will be gone before sunup. With apologies, if you'll have them."

"I'll have them," I said. "Also an explanation, which

I feel is no more than I am due."

"Don't assume to be alone in that," he said after a pause.

The rest of the evening, the cold supper we shared, the chores afterward, we spent in silence.

~~~

After feeding Aaron, checking on Mary Elizabeth, I lay awake listening to the wind. Hearing in it *Don't assume to be alone in that* and wondering at his meaning, at the choices he'd made. Two men he'd shot down. *Only adding to his total,* Longstreet made sure to mention. Yet Jubal Pyne was not the man he described. To cite evidence, there was his way with Mary Elizabeth…his speech…his manner with me. They did not reflect Longstreet's words. As if one fallen through ice and pounding for release could only appear distorted to those on the other side.

I yearned for sleep, but none came.

The excitement, I told myself.

At length I got up and looked in on Mary Elizabeth. She'd tangled in the covers, so I readjusted them, careful of her hand. I kissed her forehead, which at least felt warm despite the cold that had crept in. Thinking some leftover tapioca would help, I had some of that. But I was stalling, I knew, and after drying my hands, I put on boots and the horse blanket over my nightshift and went out to the barn.

Holding the lantern high, I searched for him and spotted Bob Lee in the stall next to our milk cow and the chicken coop. The area where our other horses would be when the ice set in.

"Mr. Pyne," I called quietly, hoping he would be asleep so that I could go back in and end this foolishness. To my right, I saw his bedroll well back in the straw, but not him.

Then a shadow moved.

"Are you alone?" he asked.

"I am."

I heard the sound of a hammer standing down, the creak of leather. Stepping into the light, he said, "Something you need?"

I took a breath, hung the lantern on a peg, caught the milk cow's placid gaze. "For one thing," I said, "you could do me the favor of accepting my apology. You are a guest in my home, and I was rude."

"You came to tell me that?"

"It needed saying. I didn't want to miss you in the morning."

He came closer, so that I was looking directly up at him. "You'll catch your death," he said.

"I'm hardly as frail as that, Mr. Pyne." I was about to add something like *much as I've seen on these plains,* but before I knew it his fingers were brushing aside the hair at my neck.

Instead of recoiling as I should have, I merely covered the tattoo.

"You mentioned respect," he said. "Try fortitude. Anyone who makes it away from the Northern Cheyenne owns it and more." And to my look, "I heard Clausen. He's a bad one, by the way."

I could say nothing, just clutch my coat tighter about me.

"You want to talk about it?" he asked.

〰️

"It wasn't Cheyenne, it was Oglala Sioux," I told him as we sat on hay bales, the light between us, his eyes on mine. "Three days from Fort Laramie they waited for our wagons. My whole family fell. We always said we'd kill ourselves, but when the time came, I could not. I lived because they liked blonde hair."

Barely conscious I was twisting a braid, a childhood habit.

"Three years I was with them, and though the beatings accorded a slave were hard, no buck ever touched me the way Clausen said."

"You survived," Jubal Pyne said. "Clausen wouldn't have."

"The tattoo denotes ownership. There'd have been more, but I pretended to faint. One day in fall, a United States soldier rode in to discuss a treaty detail. Though I was herded inside, Aaron saw me and made them an offer. As we left, him poorer by his saddle and me behind him on his mount, I kept expecting the arrows. I still expect them."

He said nothing.

"It took months to come all the way back, but a year later at Fort Sully we were married. Aaron took retirement and we moved out here." To which I added, "After too long in Spurlock."

His nod held more understanding than words.

"Mary Elizabeth keeps asking if he'll play with her again."

"What do you tell her?"

"That maybe God is waiting for Christmas."

He said, "Hope got you this far, Mrs. Van Rensslaer. Don't give it up."

"No? What about you?"

He broke off a piece of hay and chewed it. "I believe there's another side to all this and that I have to find it. That maybe it's not someplace but someone."

"I have to go," I said. "Aaron gets chilled." I'd stood and was reaching for the lamp, feeling not a little light-headed, when something made me ask, "*Were* you at Northfield?"

"I was not."

"But Longstreet said—"

"Grudges die hard in Missouri. I was at Centralia when two hundred bluecoats died, twenty-five of them unarmed."

I gasped. "You rode with Bloody Bill Anderson? Against my husband?"

"You never heard of Order Number 11? Families like mine who sympathized with the South burned out or murdered? Tell it to my wife, she was carrying our son. Why do you think there *are* Jameses and Youngers?"

"I don't know. Do you?"

He rubbed his eyes. "I was eighteen at Centralia. They had me patching up the wounded. That ended it for me."

"Then why are you here?"

"Clausen's brother died there. When he signed on with the Pinkertons, my name made Longstreet's list. Liberty, Gads Hill, Blue Cut – every robbery within three states, he had me there."

"And Independence?"

"Two of them waited for me at a livery" he said. "No warning, just that wanted poster."

"I believe I've heard enough for one day and night, thank you."

"Laney, listen to me, I don't have time to not say it. Stay tonight."

I was stunned into silence.

"Aaron's better off where they can care for him, you know that. We can make a life in Montana. California, if you want."

"Given what Aaron's meant to me, I'll pretend I didn't hear that."

"Pretend all you want," he said. "But I'm not sure I can find you a second time."

I wasn't sure the flush had risen to my face, but I

wasn't taking any chances. In haste I said, "My husband needs me, Mr. Pyne. I'll have breakfast and something for the trail at five."

And with that I hurried back inside my cold house.

〜〜
〜〜

December 21, 1879

The unseasonable weather ended that day. Morning saw the clouds thicken and by noon we had three inches of snow with more likely. I'd risen at four and had eggs and potatoes and leftover biscuits ready when Jubal Pyne knocked. Our conversation was sparse, as if what was said the night before was a dust devil that had moved on. When he finished eating, I watched him check on Mary Elizabeth then lead Bob Lee from the barn and head west.

Part of me left with him, for reasons I did not fully understand. But, of course, I did. Other than Aaron, no man had spoken to me that way, let alone triggered the feelings I had watching him go. Can one be punished for thoughts, I kept wondering, for feelings not rigorously suppressed? I was afraid of the answer.

To keep my mind where it belonged, I set to my chores, among them washing the towels we'd used tending to Mary Elizabeth. Without her help things went slowly. I was through with the wash, hanging it in the barn, when I felt a presence behind me and turned to face the proverbial arrow.

Clausen grinned. "Your kid said you might be out here."

In the dim quiet I could hear his breathing.

"You were in the house?" I said, as much incredulous as fearful.

He slapped snow off his hat, tossed it aside. "Bothers you, huh? Woman good looking as you ought to think about locks."

"What are you doing here?"

"That's for me to know and you to find out. You can start by taking off those clothes."

I looked beyond him to the door. "Where's Captain Longstreet?"

"Far enough to be of use to me and none to you. Now are you going to get to it or do I start in on your girl and that old man?"

Time...time and guilt.

"This how you repay the Pinkertons' faith in you?"

"Three dead and your place in ashes," he said, shedding his coat. Unbuckling his gun belt and letting it drop. "How long before they think your savages done it?"

My savages.

I was close enough to grab the hook from a bale and hold it in a threatening manner. By God, I would not go down without a fight.

"Fine by me," he said, grinning. "You want it hard, we do it hard."

I was agile enough to wing him to no effect before he twisted the hook and leveled me with a blow. Through stars I felt him tugging at Aaron's pants, his hardness on my leg, my shirt buttons giving way. Then his hand was inside, squeezing me until I cried out.

That was the last of him I felt.

There seemed to be two Clausens, one wrenched backward in a gloved hand. Whoever it was had him by the hair, and as I watched, drove his face into a post. Again then, and I could hear his nose break, his roar of pain as the gloved fist struck it twice more.

But Clausen wasn't done.

Pulling a knife from his boot, slashing the air with it, he backed the other off and dove for his fallen holster.

That was when Jubal Pyne drew as fast as I'd ever seen and fired.

$$\approx$$

For a long time he held me as I shook. I could feel the strength of him, the solidity, his breath in my hair as he stroked it. My face in his hands as I lost myself in the tobacco and talc and leather of him.

Rough stubble and the smell of hay.

The wind in the loft.

Finally Jubal Pyne let out a breath.

"You all right?" he asked, as though hesitant to speak.

"I'm not sure," I said, equally so. "Ask me another time."

He just nodded.

"Turn your head, please. Is Clausen dead?"

"He is."

"How–?"

"I saw him headed this way and tailed him. Bastard never even looked around."

But already my mind was a locomotive. "Longstreet valued him," I said. "He'll follow his tracks."

"The general direction, he will. But enough snow fell to cover the final miles."

The snow that now had stopped.

"Which means they'll be coming," I said.

"Which means I have work to do."

It made sense what Jubal Pyne said about disposing of him in the open; spaded snow stuck out like a crypt and the river was too low and sluggish to take a body far. Which eased my mind not at all when he buried him in the mass stall and let mares into it along with their green manure and some dried, then worked them up enough to hoof down the bulge and make it look innocent.

~~~

Three o'clock, Longstreet rode in with a crew of six.

"Looking for a man," he said. Bob Lee turned out again, Jubal Pyne somewhere in the loft with his rifle. "You remember Clausen?"

A flight of late geese honked on their way south.

"Well enough," I answered, wishing I were with them.

"Tracks indicated he might have followed through

on some things he told one of us last night. Whiskey talk, till he didn't turn up at muster."

"Haven't seen the man," I said. "No great loss to me."

His breath hung in the air. "Clausen's hewn rough, ma'am, but he knows his work."

"Not for a minute do I doubt it."

"You haven't seen him, then?"

"Trust me that I'd know, Captain."

His eyes swept the house, the barn and dugout, came to rest on the outhouse. "Any objection to our using the facility?"

"None at all," I told him, knowing he was testing me. "Long as you're gentlemen about it."

"Anybody?" he offered his men. Nodding to one in particular who got down and made his way there, drawing his pistol and holding it to his thigh before entering. Once back, exchanging looks with Longstreet, who said, "Guess we'll be going, ma'am. Your husband doing better?"

"Well as can be expected," I answered.

"Glad of it. You, too, I hope."

It caught me by surprise, too long before recognition dawned: the bruise where Clausen almost knocked me cold.

"Corral gate," I covered. "Running off a coyote.

The windmill clattered in a gust.

"Liniment's useful for swelling," he said after a look. He was turning away when he added, "By the way, I know some who'd give you a fair price for that mount of Pyne's."

"Thanks, I'll keep it in mind." Regaining my breath only when they'd scattered the ice reaching for the river's middle and crested the far bank.

≈

I was relating my exchange with Longstreet, Jubal Pyne listening without comment, when Mary Elizabeth appeared in her nightgown and held out her bandage.

Her bandage. In all that had happened, I'd forgotten to change it.

"Mama it hurts. A really lot."

"I know sweetheart," I said. "You're mama's brave girl."

"Then you're not mad at me?"

"How could I be mad at you for making me a present?"

"Mr. Smith isn't mad I didn't make him one?"

"Mr. Smith is just glad to see you on your feet," he

told her.

"Papa is too," she answered brightly. "He told me so."

A chill gripped me. Aaron, to my knowledge, was the same as he'd been since July, neither a wave of the hand nor a syllable. Trying to keep the urgency from my voice, I said, "Papa told you this? When?"

"Just now, when he told me to show you my hand."

I checked Aaron: no change. Around my heart in my mouth, I said, "Come here," and felt Mary Elizabeth's cheek.

The skin was as warm as her hand was swollen.

≋

After I'd set her hand in warm water, iodine, and Epsom salts, I sat staring at the snow falling outside while Jubal Pyne made coffee. Handing me mine, he said, "If you're blaming yourself, don't. It was the blade. I've seen enough to know."

"And?"

"I won't lie to you about blood poisoning."

"Lord help us. Are you sure?"

"You saw the line starting up her wrist?"

Tears welled. I felt his hand on mine and in my state

left it there.

"It's early," he said. "I've seen the salts work, too."

I searched his eyes. "When can you tell?"

"Morning, I expect."

<center>~~~</center>

We passed the night in shifts, Jubal Pyne insisting I rest, perhaps seeing a line rising in me, too, each of us trying to keep Mary Elizabeth's hand in the solution. Which was a hard row as restless as she was, whimpering in fevered sleep. As for me, I slept not at all during the shifts that were his, just lay in bed praying and mulling over thoughts of remorse and penance.

Tick-tock intruded the clock on the mantel.

Normally my ally in sleep, it now only made the night longer.

Toward morning, Mary Elizabeth sat up and asked, "Will he be hungry?"

"Who'll be hungry, sweetheart?"

"Papa when he wakes up."

"No sweetheart, he'll be fine," I told her. "That's why we feed him."

"I'm glad, mama."

"I'm glad you're glad."

"Mama?" Her brown eyes beseeching mine from under the cloth I'd laid on her forehead to cool it. "Please make it stop hurting."

December 22, 1879

By mid-morning the sky was the mottle of tarnished silver. Snow lay against the barn and had nearly obliterated the sod dugout. I'd just finished feeding Aaron his potato soup, reading to him afterward, my mind on Mary Elizabeth, when I sensed Jubal Pyne standing where I'd first seen him in the house, in Aaron's doorway. Now it would have been unexpected had he *not* been there.

I said, "You're wondering why I read to him, aren't you?"

"Have to say it crossed my mind," he answered.

"He can hear me, I know he can. It's what I meant by not in the usual sense."

A moment went by. Then, "Any objection if I smoke?"

I shook my head and he lit a cigarette he'd already rolled.

"One thing I do know," he said, exhaling. "If Aaron can hear you, anyone can."

Tired as I was and in no mood to opine who'd been receiving my prayers of late, which I assumed was his point, I said nothing. A moment went by as he focused on Aaron's face, the book in my hands.

"You get any rest?"

"Enough," I said.

Wind howled down the chimney and around the sashes.

"I hope so," he said.

〜〜〜

Jubal Pyne looked up from the wood, which hissed and popped where he'd laid it. Yet beyond the fire's radius, the cold prevailed with a vengeance, Aaron's hot water bottles lasting only short intervals before needing filling again.

"Line's risen a good inch since last night," he said regarding Mary Elizabeth, visible through her open door. "No news to you."

I assured him I had eyes, thank you.

"Laney, there's only so much we can do here. She needs a doctor."

"It's early, you said so yourself."

His expression remained unchanged.

"Long as you're on what's needed, a break in the storm would be nice," I snapped. Then, after a breath, "Sorry. I'd be obliged if you'd hitch up the wagon so I can take her in."

"Wagon won't make it without a road to follow."

I said, "Then I'll saddle one of the mares."

"Thirty miles. In ice and snow." And when I'd not responded, "Bob Lee and I stand the best chance."

From the way he said it, the only chance.

"You forgetting the Pinkertons?" I asked. "Where they're likely holed up in this?"

"You see them catch me so far?"

"I'll ride Bob Lee."

"He's too much horse. He's not used to you."

"In a few miles he will be."

"You won't make it. Which means the three of you."

Taking a breath, having admitted this to no one – and I mean *no* one – I said, "I lost a son waiting too long. Do you think I'd risk my daughter by–" I had to stop and compose myself.

"I'm going. You're not. That's it."

"And what of Aaron?" he said.

"Feed him every four hours. Keep him warm."

"You'd trust your husband to me after–"

"Yes," I said, looking him square in the eye.

He hunched over to light another cigarette. When he rose up his face had hardened into the one I'd first seen aboard Bob Lee.

"I lied to you," he said. "Every bank and train Longstreet has me up for I was there. I've killed more men than you can count. You think I'd let one more stand in my way?"

"I'll be saddling the gray," I said. "Wrap Elizabeth for me, will you?"

Throwing the cigarette in the fire, he took a Peacemaker from its holster and started for Aaron's room. He had a pillow over Aaron's face, the barrel to it and the hammer back, when I screamed, *No! Don't!*

"Watch me. Better yet, give me a reason."

"You can't." And before I knew it, *"I love you."*

"Then you're a bigger fool than I thought. Take off the blinders, a man like me only wants one thing from a woman."

By then I could hardly see.

"You're not like that. You had a wife. You had children."

"That was a kid I served with who died. Once a thief, right?" His grin was a blade. "There, you all right *now?* As I recall, you wanted me to ask."

I could only stand there.

"You can do better than that, Mrs. Van Rensslaer. Speak up."

"I hate you," I said.

"Say it again."

"*I hate you.*"

For a moment that seemed like forever, I could hear my heart pounding. Later, as Bob Lee left the barn and headed toward the river, Mary Elizabeth a mere bulge inside Jubal Pyne's coat, I allowed myself a look. But only then.

$$\sim\!\!\sim$$

December 25, 1879

The days before Christmas were a blur. Snow fell on and off, the temperature as if there were no bottom.

Christmas Eve, I crawled in beside Aaron and held him, and in the process warmed us both enough to give the water bottles a rest. I even thought he moved a little. Finally the 25th dawned as if the weather meant the day to be a gift: calm and bright.

I'd shoveled my way to the barn and was milking the cow around midday when I heard a hail and went outside to find Doc Stroebel in his rig, the most welcome sight beside him on the seat.

"Mama," Mary Elizabeth said, getting down and wading toward me. *"I'm back."* And as I picked her up and held her, being careful of her new bandage, "Why are you crying? I'm fine now."

As she skipped toward the house, Doc handed me a box with a roast dinner his wife had fixed us. Saying to my thanks, "Men I know will be here tomorrow to chop wood and such, whatever you need. And the man who paid for Mary Elizabeth wanted you to have this."

The sack held more double-eagles than I'd seen all year.

I was afraid to ask, but I did. "This man, he get away all right?"

"Course not, you wouldn't have heard. Pinkertons gunned him, recognized his horse outside the saloon.

Some big outlaw they'd been chasing." And with a look at me over his spectacles, "If you can picture an outlaw going in to get drunk in a town full of Pinkertons. After delivering what he did."

Ice ran in my veins. I could neither move nor speak.

Doc touched my arm. "Figured you had enough on your plate without me volunteering to them why he'd come, and from where."

Then, with a look at the house, Mary Elizabeth bounding about, "A gift is only a gift when you accept it, Laney. Don't make it less."

"Doc, I–"

"Change her dressing often, there's ointment in the box. Oh, and that Pinkerton on his way out of town asked me to give you this." Reaching into a pocket for it. "Said you'd know what it meant."

Folded into the wanted poster were bank notes and a sheet with handwriting I decided read: One sorrel roan in the amount of $100, freely transacted this day of our Lord, 25 December 1879. Underlined was, No further consideration required.

It was signed William Longstreet.

After Doc checked Aaron he was anxious to get back, so I thanked him again for Mary Elizabeth and the food and all, then watched until his rig was a black speck against the snow. Out there beyond the river.

Until the wind picked up and I went inside.

~~~

Aaron rallied that spring, but he was never the same. And yet, we were happy. After a trip that's another story, we made it to California, where we got into the laundry business, then the hotel business, our own before he died. Mary Elizabeth is a doctor in Salt Lake and our son Jubal was just made an adjutant under General Pershing at the Presidio.

Still, despite our turn of fortune, the white cloths and the silver and the crystal, I now and then take out the double eagle I refused to spend even when things got tight.

And I hold it. And I hear the wind again.

The way it gets inside a person and won't come out.

Three thousand hardcover copies of *Wind on the River* were printed by Capra Press. Fifty copies have been numbered and signed by the author and Mr. Coben. Twenty-six copies in slipcases were also lettered and signed by both.

If you enjoyed *Wind on the River*, don't miss the first and second in Richard Barre's Christmas series:

The Star

In L.A.'s threatening Crenshaw district of 1952, Byron Whitaker is given a Christmas gift he will never forget – from a mysterious silent-movie star with his greatest role yet to play. With a foreward by Michael Connelly, author of *The Narrows* and *Last Light*.

Bethany

Frank Shane is big-rigging a night run of Christmas trees through a blizzard when he encounters the last thing he expects. Or does he? Second in the series, Bethany includes a foreword by Robert Crais, author of *L.A. Requiem* and *The Last Detective*.

To order, contact Capra Press at 805-892-2722 or log onto www.caprapress.com.

About Capra Press

Capra Press was founded in 1969 by the late Noel Young. Among its authors have been Henry Miller, Ross Macdonald, Margaret Millar, Edward Abbey, Anais Nin, Raymond Carver, Ray Bradbury, and Lawrence Durrell. It is in this tradition that we present the new Capra: literary and mystery fiction, lifestyle and city books. Contact us. We welcome your comments.

815 De La Vina Street, Santa Barbara, CA 93101
805-892-2722; www.caprapress.com